A Book About a Boy

Kendra Cuzick

DEDICATION

This is for you, Jackson.
And for every child who has struggled in school.

CHAPTERS

ACKNOWLEDGMENTS

Thank you, Mrs. Flores, for believing in Jackson and helping him believe in himself. Thank you, Mrs. Johnston, for making school enjoyable. And my dear Jackson, thank you for being my boy.

CHAPTER ONE

I'm different.

I don't look different, but I am.

I can feel it.

One day in class my teacher asked us what we had learned that year. I told her "nothing". I really hadn't learned anything I didn't already know. She didn't believe me. I got in trouble.

Mom said there is always something to learn. Even if we already know something, there is always more we can learn. If you know how to read you can read more challenging books. If you know how to write you can learn different writing styles. If you know math you can learn to do more complicated math.

My problem isn't with math. That's easy. My problem is reading. And writing. "Well, didn't you learn to do it better?" asked Mom. I should have said yes. Most kids would say yes. But I can't. I didn't learn how to read or write any better than I had the year before. Or the year before that.

Nobody believes me when I say, I can't read.

Dear Mrs. Jones,

Jackson is having a hard time not wanting to go to school. I was wondering how he is doing this week. Has anything at school changed that might make him feel uncomfortable?

Thank you,

Mrs. C

CHAPTER TWO

I'm Jackson. I will be starting 4th grade after

summer. I'm glad it's summer, and I don't have to go

back to school. School's hard. I hate it. I don't know

why they make me go. I already know everything.

Third grade was horrible.

I live in Arizona. I live in a house that's on a dirt

road. It's a nice house with a huge backyard. Dad likes

the house but is tired of dirt roads. Mom and I don't mind them. Although dirt roads do make riding my bike hard.

It's so hot in the summer. We don't have our own pool so we like to turn the sprinklers on in the backyard and go on the slip n slide instead. We used to do it a lot, but we are getting a little big.

One time we invited lots of friends over to play on the slip n slide. We played for hours. When we finished the grass was flooded! The other moms were worried but Mom and Dad just said, "It'll dry." And it did.

I'm doing swim team this summer. I like doing swim team. I'm good at it. Although I hate jumping in the water for the first time. It's always cold. My first time doing swim team was the summer before I started kindergarten. Mom had to throw me in the pool every day because I refused to jump in by myself. If there wasn't a coach nearby to force me to swim I would climb out, and Mom would throw me right back in. Some days we did this several times until a coach came and pulled me away from the edge. I was fine after that. I recently told Mom I used to do that because the water was cold. She laughed and said, "Is that why? Well, you had me fooled. I thought you were scared."

I don't mind swimming or competing, but I'm always nervous on the first swim meet. I make Mom walk me to our team's spot. I make her ask the coach my questions and I make her stay where I can see her. After my first meet I always feel pretty good about myself and Mom doesn't have to stay so close.

I like my coach. He works us hard but at the end we play games, like sharks and minnows. Sometimes my coach will walk past a kid and toss them in the pool just for fun. I didn't do swim team last year so I was nervous starting this summer, but my coach makes it a lot of fun.

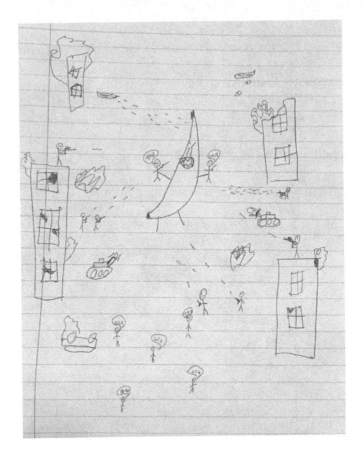

Dear Mrs. Jones,

Jackson loved school for the first part of this school year, but is now back to his usual "I hate school" attitude. I'm really concerned that his lack of confidence in reading is causing a lot of anxiety for him. Do you have suggestions on how I can give him extra help?

Mrs. C

CHAPTER THREE

I have an older brother, Harrison, and a younger

sister, Lucy. Sometimes we have fun together, and

sometimes they are so annoying. One time we were

driving to school when Lucy farted. Harrison said

"I sense a disturbance in the force" like he was Darth

Vader in Star Wars. I still laugh about that.

Harrison is eleven and has dark brown hair and wears glasses. He will be in sixth grade when school starts again. He loves to read. That's all he does, all the time. When he's not reading he's talking about Pokémon. I wish he would just play with me.

Lucy is seven. She has blond hair and blue eyes and will be in second grade. She is so annoying. She is always coming into my bedroom without asking. Mom says she just wants to play but all she does is make a mess.

I have blondish brownish hair and brown eyes. Mom says my eyes look more yellow than brown. She also says I look like a surfer boy with my wavy hair. I wear glasses too.

We aren't doing a lot this summer, except

packing. That's because we are moving. Or trying to. We can't seem to sell our house even though we painted and ripped out all the flooring to put new tile and carpet in. We've made all kinds of changes and people are coming to look at our house, but nobody wants to buy it yet. Dad says it will take the right person. Whenever someone comes to look at our house we run around like crazy making sure it looks nice. Then we pile into the car, with our dog and everyone, and drive around. We can't really go anywhere because we have our dog with us and it's too hot to go to the park.

Dad says we will probably have to move out before it sells. I don't want to move. I like our house. I have lived here my whole life. I don't like change.

Some change is ok. One big change is that
Mom's having a baby. It's a boy. As long as he doesn't
cry, I'm excited.

We call the baby "Blueberry". When Mom and
Dad told us we were going to have a new baby we
asked how big he was. Mom has an app on her phone
that tells her each week how big the baby is. That
week he was the size of a blueberry. That's how he
got his nickname. We don't have a real name yet. I
like the name Ford. Mom does too, but she says she
can't name her oldest child Harrison and her youngest
child Ford. Put them together and you get Harrison
Ford, the actor who played Han Solo in Star Wars
(my favorite movie).

Every week Mom looks on the baby app on her
phone and tells us how big the baby is. Right now

he's about as big as a GI Joe toy, whatever that is. I can't wait until he's the size of a watermelon.

Mom's been sick a lot with being pregnant. She doesn't cook very much anymore and she spends a lot of time resting on the couch. We have started eating out a lot, especially at the beginning when she was really sick. It was fun for a little while but we are all tired of it, and are ready to have dinner like normal.

Mom said there are some families who never make and eat dinner together. Some families don't ever eat together, and some families always eat out. I'm glad we don't. I'm glad Mom makes dinner and we eat together as a family. I'm ready for Mom to feel good again so we can do that all the time like before. We only have a couple of months left. The Blueberry is due in August, right before school starts.

Mrs. C,

I hope you are doing well. I wanted to touch base with you about how Jackson has been doing. I have seen him take more of a leadership role lately. He does this in many ways including un-stacking the chairs for all those in his group and other groups in the morning.

Yesterday and today Jackson has had a difficult time getting motivated. Yesterday he was more reserved than usual and was unwilling to follow directions on an assignment. When I asked him to go back and check his work to complete the directions he was very reluctant and when he did rework only added a few words. Again, I asked him to show his best work and he said that he was. I talked with him about how smart I know he is and that I want him to be able to show proof of that in his work. I had him stop and asked him to revisit his assignment today. Jackson did come in and complete his work this morning which was great.

Then, when I was checking agendas he had crossed out my smile face and put a sad face. I met with him to ask why or what was going on and he said he was sad. When I asked why he said he didn't know. I reminded him we are here to help and if he wanted to talk I was here for him. I also brought this to Mr. Woods' attention (our school psychologist). He was able to do a check-in with Jackson today. Jackson did share with Mr. Woods that you are in the process of officially moving. Knowing Jackson I understand that this can be frustrating for him as it is not his normal routine.

I am glad he was able to share this with Mr. Woods. We will be on the lookout for anything else in class. I just wanted you to know that Jackson has been out of character and I was concerned. If you have any questions or concerns please let me know and I will do the same.

Mrs. Jones

CHAPTER FOUR

With getting ready to move and getting ready for the baby we will probably spend most of our summer at home. We used to go do things like go to the Science Center (which I love) or the library (which I hate). Sometimes we would go to Chuck E Cheese just to play the games. I'm ok with not doing so much. I really just want to be home and away from school. I like being home. I don't like being at school. Nobody understands me. Everyone makes me so mad. I don't understand how everyone in class can get their work done and I can't, even though I'm smarter than they are. I don't feel smart at school. I can't read or write and everything we do is reading and writing. There are no fun projects or science experiments. I like science and social studies. I wish I could learn about that. Instead we just do worksheets of stuff I already know. But my teacher gets mad and I get in trouble when I don't do my work. I don't know why I need to do it when I already know it. They want me to show my work but that's what I can't do. They don't understand that I can't read, I can't spell, and nobody can read my handwriting, sometimes not even me.

I like the summer. Sometimes at home we do science experiments or have shaving cream wars. We get cans of shaving cream and run around the yard spraying each other. At the end we're covered in shaving cream. Then we get the hose and play in the water, washing each other off.

I have time to myself in the summer. I get to do the things that I want to do, like play Legos. The other day I created my own nation. I made a document and called it "The Jacksonation of Independence". I don't think I spelled it right. I made my document look old and rolled it up like a scroll.

Mom is taking me to a special doctor who is having me do all kinds of tests. I don't mind because the doctor has a dog named Moose. Moose is super soft and loves his tennis ball. I get to pet him and play with him while I'm taking my tests. I was a little bummed about seeing this doctor because I had to miss my first day of swim team but it wasn't that bad. Moose made it better.

The tests I took weren't reading and writing tests. They were different. They were challenging. I like to be challenged. I felt like they wanted to see how smart I was instead of just doing what they tell me to do. It was a long day but I had breaks and I had Moose.

I like to doodle, even though I'm horrible at drawing. This one says, "Welcome to Happy Land." You can go there to get free Chick fil A (Mom told me how to spell that). In Happy Land you can get ice cream from Mr. Banana Ice Cream and chocolate from the chocolate pond.

Mr. Woods

I am concerned about my son, Jackson. Jackson is in third grade and is not only struggling with reading but has a low self-esteem and high anxiety. Reading has always been a struggle for him and has recently become more frustrating because his first grade sister now reads better than he does. He is very critical of himself and has high anxiety. Because of these concerns, and others, I wonder if there is something prohibiting his learning of reading, such as dyslexia.

Is there anything you or the school can do to help Jackson? I'm at a loss on how to help him.

Mrs. C.

CHAPTER FIVE

I finished my first swim meet. I did surprisingly well. I actually didn't want to do swim team this year because I'm old enough that I have to do flip turns. I didn't know how to and that made me nervous. Mom said that's why we have practice and coaches, so we can learn. Dad said he doesn't know how to do flip turns either and we can learn together. So, despite not knowing how to do flip turns I still got second place on my very first race!

My little sister, Lucy, didn't race. This is her first year doing swim team and she's scared. I told her she's not going to stop being scared if she doesn't try. Mom isn't making her race. I don't know why. She made me race when it was my first year of swim team. Oh well, I got a ribbon and she didn't.

Mom's getting anxious. She wants to get ready for the baby. But we're still trying to sell our house and she can't set up the baby's room when we aren't going to be living there. I'm not sure why we are moving. Mom and Dad say it will be good for us. I like our house. But there aren't a lot of kids in our neighborhood. Mom and Dad want to live in a neighborhood where we have kids to play with and they want us to be able to walk to school and ride our bikes. The plan is to sell our house and live in a rental house until the house sells. Then we can buy a new one.

It's getting so close to having the baby. Mom likes the idea of renting while we wait for our house to sell because she can get the crib set up and all ready for the baby. Plus, we will be settled before school starts.

I'm not ready to think about going back to school. I just finished third grade. It was the worst year of my life. I got in trouble just for asking a question. And when I got frustrated and ripped up my paper I would get sent to the principal's office. They would send my work to the principal's office where I was supposed to finish it. Doing my work in the office didn't make it easier to do. Office or classroom, I still couldn't do it.

We went back to the doctor. He gave us my test scores. He said I have the mind of a Ferrari. I like that. He said I'm a speed racer not a marathon runner. I guess it means I can work really well for a short amount of time. He said I was smart. Above average. I know that I'm smarter than most people in my class at school but they can do their work. I can't. They can go to school and not get into trouble. I can't.

The doctor said I have dyslexia and dysgraphia. I'm not sure what that means but Mom said now we know why reading is hard and now I can get the right help. Mom talked with the doctor for a long time. After he talked to me I got to go play with Moose. I like Moose. He's so soft and fluffy.

When we got home Mom explained what dyslexia is. I still don't fully understand. Dyslexia is a disorder in my brain. My brain doesn't match letters with their sounds like other brains do. So when it comes to reading my brain can't figure out the words. My brain reads and writes and spells differently than other kids. But I'm not alone. A lot of people have dyslexia. Walt Disney was dyslexic. Mom says I'm going to grow up to be another Walt Disney. I'm very creative and clever she says. I could handle being like Walt Disney, making movies and building a theme park with rollercoasters. I love rollercoasters. The faster the better. I also like making movies. I make stop motion movies using my iPad and army men.

Mrs. Jones,

Jackson is having a rough week. He complains and begs not to go back to school. We have had many conversations and I know he appreciated his talk with Mr. Wood.

He feels he is not liked and can't do anything right. I don't understand why he feels this way and why he takes any criticism so personally.

He also says school is too easy and he knows everything so he doesn't even pay attention because he is so bored. But then he says he is always being told what to do because he doesn't do his work.

He is a riddle that I can't figure out!

Mrs. C.

CHAPTER SIX

Even though we are trying to move we do get to go on a vacation this summer. We get to go to Lake Powell. We are staying on a houseboat with my grandparents, aunts and uncles, and my cousins. Lake Powell is the best. Red rocks, cold green water, swimming, boating, knee boarding, fishing, paddle boarding. I could stay there all summer. We go almost every year. I like when we ride the speed boat. I sit in the very front of the boat so the wind can blow in my face. I like going fast. When it gets hot we take a break and go for a swim. The water is so cold it takes me a little while to jump in. I try to get in by myself before Dad throws me in. Lucy never gets thrown in. She's always the first one in the water. She doesn't mind cold water. Harrison doesn't ways get in. Sometimes he stays in the boat. Mom didn't swim much either. It's too hard for her to get on and off the boat with her big belly. She hasn't ridden the boats very much at all. She said the bumpy boat ride hurts her belly.

Every time we go to Lake Powell we take a really long boat ride. We stop at Dangling Rope Marina for fuel and ice cream. We also feed the fish. They swarm and fight over anything they think is food. They will even eat your spit. Harrison and I like to spit into the lake and watch the fish eat it. Dad said Dangling Rope was given that name because when people found it there was only one rope dangling from the cliffs. I'm not sure he's telling the truth. Dad likes to tease.

I like to tease also. I really like to tease Lucy. Sometimes she laughs when I tease. Harrison doesn't laugh, he gets mad. Nobody gets mad when Dad teases, which is a lot. We always look at Mom's expression to tell if he's joking or telling the truth. Even when we know he is joking Dad will go on and on, making us laugh.

Mom likes to read and write. I don't understand

how she can do it. I have so many ideas that I wish I could write but I can't get my thoughts on paper. And when I do I can't read what I wrote. I love books, or would if I could read them. I want to know everything that is in them. Mom reads to me a lot. At night we all climb into Mom and Dad's bed and Mom reads to us kids. We are reading Summer of the Monkeys. It is so funny. I beg Mom to read more but she will only read one chapter at a time. After Mom reads to us she says good night and sends us to bed. She says we get to tuck her in. I think she is too tired with being pregnant to tuck us in. So after we've played around hiding under the covers and stuff we tuck her in and say goodnight.

Mom writes stories for us. She reads them to us and asks our opinions. She worked on one for a really long time. When she finished she read it to us. I wish I could write.

I saw the Lego set I have been wanting. I was hoping to buy it but I didn't have enough money. I wasn't even close. Harrison gave me money from his birthday so I could buy it. Sometimes I really like Harrison.

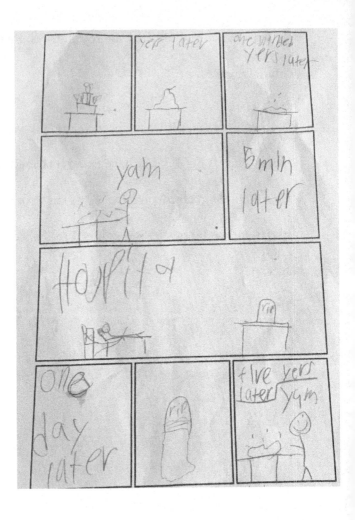

Dear Mrs. C.

I just want to give an update on how Jackson's week was. I have been working on having him communicate his needs and thoughts as he often says, "I don't know" or does not respond at all. As I mentioned before I am working on showcasing him when I now he knows a vocabulary term or more information on a topic. This has helped bring him out of his shell a bit. I have also been observing his socialization or interactions with his peers in class and he is still doing well with his group. I have been asking more about scouts and I have found a connection with him through Star Wars. I know you will appreciate my humor and that I got him to laughed out loud when I said, "may the force be with your pencil." That was a joy to hear!

Today Jackson was a bit more reserved and became more withdrawn towards the end of the day. He was one of many who did not return his homework and I made a deal with all of them to turn it in on Monday so that they could enjoy some class earned free time. Jackson wasn't willing to agree to bring in his homework and Monday. I said he could have time to think about it. I know that when he has time to process he can communicate his needs or thoughts further. Many of my students checked on him when he was sitting at his desk and he wrote "go away" to convey that he wanted to be left alone. I did talk with him about saying "please may I have some alone time?" or "may I have some space?". I wanted him to know that everyone cares about him and how he is doing and that is why they were asking how he was.

I was thinking about seeing if there is room in Mrs. Snow's socialization group. She does some excellent exercises in helping students learn how to share their ideas and feelings. If you would like that please let me know and I will ask if there is room. Mr. Woods has also made himself available to speak with Jackson if needed but Jackson did not want to this week when I asked him if he needed that time. I truly want what is best for him and what will help him feel successful at school. As always, please let me know if you have any questions.

Thank you,

Mrs. Jones

CHAPTER SEVEN

We got to go to Wet n Wild. It's a super fun water park. I like the big fast slides. Dad and Lucy like them too. Harrison doesn't like them but we make him go with us anyway. We had fun but had to go home early because it started to rain. I wanted to stay until it closed. But I loved it anyway.

We have looked and looked and looked and finally found a house we are going to live in. Looking at houses is so boring. We had to look at too many. Officially moving means we have more packing to do. We have already packed so much. There are boxes everywhere. We are all tired of it and ready to be done. I wish we could just not pack and stay in our house.

One good thing about moving is I will be closer to my friend. I have one friend. Aaron. We weren't in the same class in third grade. I hope we will be in the same class in fourth. We didn't meet until December. And we didn't even meet at school. We met at a church Christmas party. The first half of third grade felt very lonely without a friend. I didn't have any friends because we are at a new school. We started going to the new school because we want our new house to be by the new school. When I say new I mean new. It's a brand new school so it's new to everyone. Mom said I shouldn't be worried because everyone was new. But I still was. At least I have a friend now. My Mom's glad I have a friend and Aaron's mom is glad he has a friend. I'm glad I have a friend too.

Aaron helped me draw a dragon to go with my guy roasting marshmallows. He uses the dragon's fiery breath to do it. I can't decide what caption to use with my picture. "A better way to roast a marshmallow." " My way's better than your way." "There's more than one way to roast a marshmallow." "I like this way more." Or, "That's one way to do that."

Dear Mrs. Jones,

Jackson has had a rough couple of weeks. He claims everyday was a bad day and begs not to go to school. I'm trying to get to the root of the problem. He says he is always being told what to do and his picked on. We have talked about the reason he goes to school is to learn and improve and it's the teacher's job to help him do that. Doing the work correctly and following all directions is how you know he is learning. I think Mrs. Snow's group would be helpful. I would also like him to continue talking to Mr. Woods. If there is anything you can think of that we can do at home please let me know.

Mrs. C.

CHAPTER EIGHT

We moved. It was a long, hot, hard day. And it lasted forever. We started really early. It was still so hot at 6:30 in the morning. Mom and Dad bought lots of doughnuts and Popsicles for everyone who helped us. I think I had three doughnuts and I don't even know how many Popsicles. The good thing about moving is our rental house has a swimming pool so at least we can swim when it gets too hot. Now we have to unpack. We are so tired of this packing/unpacking thing. It's all Mom has been doing. We all just want a break!

Sometimes Mom and I go see a lady that we have to talk to. I guess she's a counselor. Sometimes I talk to her by myself. Sometimes Mom talks to her. Sometimes we talk to her together. She tries to help me not get so angry. I don't mean to get angry. I don't want to. I just get mad and lose control. I went to school every day thinking I was going to make it a good day. But I still got sent to the principal a lot for getting mad. And I still couldn't do my work. The doctor we went to see earlier in the summer said it's not my fault. That my intentions are good but there is something in my mind that doesn't do what I want to do. He said it's my executive functions. That's the part of the brain that helps us do important things like not get mad and to organize and set goals. I don't totally understand. Mom and my counselor try to help me understand and to stay in control and remember the things I'm supposed to do. One day I walked out of my room and went to put my shoes on. Mom asked me why I wasn't going to change my clothes in my bedroom. I looked in my hand and there were my clothes. I got them out and forgot to change into them! I get easily distracted.

I might not be good at some things but I'm good at making people laugh. I went up to Mom, saluted and said, "Permission to use the bathroom so I can do my duty."

We had our last swim meet, it was regionals. I made it to regionals! That's the good thing. The bad thing is that it was outside in Arizona in July. I had to wait my turn to swim. It's was so hot. I couldn't wait to swim to cool off. I did alright. I didn't get first but I'm happy anyway.

We went to the lake. We only went for a few hours after Dad finished work. But any day on the lake is always a good day. And it was nice to take a break from packing and unpacking. I always sit at the front of the boat when Dad drives fast. It makes my hair go wild. I love driving fast. I also love going on the inner tube. The faster and crazier the better. Dad is teaching me how to kneeboard. I'm getting pretty good at it.

I have a dog named Barkley. He's a black standard poodle with a mohawk. Barkley is a good dog but sometimes he runs out when the front door is open, then it's hard to get him back. It didn't matter so much in our old house. We didn't have a fence and

neither did most of our neighbors. With the dirt road

there weren't a lot of cars so it was ok if Barkley got

out. In our new rental house it's not ok. There are

more people and cars and paved streets. He got

out and we had to go chase him. He ran so far it was

hard to catch him. Some neighbor kids came to help.

That was nice of them.

The other day Lucy said, "Barkley I'm going to

marry you" Then Harrison said, "you can't marry

Barkley or you will have werewolves. And then they

will run amuck". They would definitely run amuck

with a dad like Barkley. I got Barkley for my 8th

birthday. I was so lonely and wanted a friend. He is a

good friend. He likes to play but he also likes to

snuggle. And he likes soft toys. He carries them in his

mouth all the time. Barkley loves people. He gets so excited when people come over. He goes crazy jumping on them. Sometimes he gets so excited he pees.

1. you now How 2 heds are
   beter then one wot abot
   3 Heds

2. if you wer dom and
   you got anothep Hed
   wod you becom avrige or
   ne twis as dom

3. if I eat my self wod I becom
   twis as big nor disipear intirly

4. if a vegitarin becam zomby
   wod ne eat vegetabls or branes

5. for raneders to fly das it hav
   to be raneing

6. das sunta have the soper
   power to not get disavedys

7. wen a pen deis das it becom
   a pensoll

1. You know how 2 heads are better than one? What about 3 heads?

2. If you were dumb and you got another head would you become average or be twice as dumb?"

3. If I eat myself would I become twice as big or disappear entirely?"

4. If a vegetarian become a zombie would he eat vegetables or brains?"

5. For reindeers to fly does it have to be raining?

6. Does Santa have the superpower to not get diabetes?

7. When a pen dies does it become a pen-soul?

Hi Mrs. C.

I just wanted to let you know that Jackson had a rough day at school today. I'm not sure if it was because he was still not feeling well from the flu or if he just wasn't wanting to participate. Hi teacher, Mrs. Jones, called the school psychologist, Mr. Woods, up to try and talk to Jackson because he had completely shut down, with his head on his desk and refusing to do any work or leave the classroom. Mr. Woods went to observe him and talk to him, but he would not interact with him at all today. I was asked to come in and support and I spoke with Jackson and was able to eventually get him to come down to the front office and talk to me about what was going on, but it took a lot of coaxing. Myself and our principal both tried to talk to him and ask him how he was feeling and what we could do to help. He wouldn't say much, but kept shrugging his shoulders. We tried to have him help us come up with some incentives he could earn (like Star Wars stuff, etc.) and he said he didn't care about anything. We had his work brought up to the front office and tried to get him to work on it, but he refused. He brought it all home with him for homework.

I feel so bad that Jackson seems down and not liking school. He did so great with me last week in social skills group. I think Mrs. Jones is really concerned as am I and our principal. We really want to help Jackson in any way possible and want him to enjoy coming to school and learning. Can we schedule a team meeting to discuss all of this sometime next week? Thank you so much and have a good evening.

Mrs. Snow

CHAPTER NINE

Now that we are moved in we got to go school shopping. Mom gave us our supply list and let us do our own shopping. Lucy and Harrison wanted all the expensive things. I only got the things I really need. I'm not looking forward to going back to school. There were some things I hated about third grade. Music class, assemblies, reading class, all the mean kids and other things. I felt so frustrated with school, Mom finally started tutoring me during my class reading time. I was so glad to see her every day. I was so glad the principal let Mom tutor me at school. We would work for most of the time, then at the end we would play games or mom would read to me. Mom was convinced I had dyslexia. That's why she got me tested. She was right.

It's the end of summer break. School starts too soon in Arizona. It's only the first of August and school starts next week. I guess we technically have one week left of summer but Mom is having the baby in two days so summer break's pretty much over. We are all excited to have a new baby. Mom was sick a lot and spent a lot of time laying on the couch or sleeping, when she wasn't packing or unpacking. Even though I could tell she didn't feel good she still helped me. Like the time we had to take our state standardized tests. I got to the reading part and just couldn't do it. I couldn't sit still. They said I was distracting the other students. They made me go to the office to take the test even though I wanted to stay in my classroom. Being in the office didn't help. I still couldn't do it. The principal called my mom. She came to the school and sat with me and the teacher. They tried to get me to finish. It took all day but finally at the end of the day I did it. It was so hard. I was happy to have Mom next to me. When Dad heard about it he said on my next test I could go home as soon as I finished. The next day was math. I don't mind math. They still made me do my testing in the front office. I finished in less than two hours. Mom picked me up. I spent the rest of the day at home.

I have a new baby brother! His name is Calvin. I'm not so sure about the name. It was Mom's grandpa's name, so I guess it's ok. Calvin is squishy and has lots of hair and is so squishy. I like him.

We got to bring Calvin home from the hospital. It's weird calling him Calvin because he has always been Blueberry. Tonight, after we got home, Dad took us to the school for meet the teacher. Now that we live so close and Mom can't drive yet we get to ride our bikes. Dad is riding with us to meet the teacher so we will be ready to do it on our own when school starts on Monday. I will be starting 4th grade. Lucy will be in 2nd and Harrison in 6th. I want to do good. I want to learn. But I'm nervous. Kids in my class were mean and my teacher didn't understand.

But I want to learn.

Dad went to a meeting at the school. Mom usually goes and wanted to but because of Calvin Dad had to go alone. They talked about my classroom accommodations. I guess they read my doctor's report so they know I have dyslexia. They say they know how to help me now and the doctor gave them some good ideas. I don't know if their good ideas are going to be any good for me.

Mrs. Jones,

I did a lot of research last week and spoke with a specialist and I think Jackson has dyslexia. I am going to have him tested. Unfortunately, it will take a few weeks but I think it will be beneficial. I have also found a tutoring program that I think will help. I'm just trying to decide if I can tutor him (this program teaches me how) or if I should have the specialist tutor him (she uses the same program).

What you your thoughts? Do you see any symptoms of dyslexia?

Thank you,

Mrs. C.

CHAPTER TEN

Today was the first day of school. My friend,
Aaron, is in my class! It was a good first day. It was
even better when we got home and had our back to
school party. Every year on the first day of school
Mom has balloons and a special treat waiting for us
when we get home. None of us thought we would
have our party this year because the baby is only five
days old. We were so surprised when we came in the
house from riding our bikes home and saw balloons
and caramel corn waiting for us. Maybe it will be a

good year.

Every night after school we have been watching the Olympics. They are in Brazil this year. Dad loves the Olympics and I do too. We like to talk about going to the winter Olympics in Japan. We also like to talk about what event we would do if we were Olympians. I would swim. We love to laugh at the ping pong players. They say it's table tennis but we all know it's ping pong. And it's hilarious. They get all set up to do this grand serve and then barely tap that little ball. There are so many events I could watch all day and I would if I wasn't in school.

School's hard. It's better than last year but it's still hard. I'm getting help with reading. Mrs. Flores teaches me. I go to her room every day with another boy in my class. I like being in her class. When I get angry or frustrated I'm allowed to take a break and walk down to her room. She always has something for me to do. Like clean the whiteboard or sharpen pencils. I visit her a lot.

Taking breaks is one of my accommodations. There are other things that are supposed to help like being given more time to take tests. It's all in my IEP plan, individualized education plan. I don't want a plan. I don't want accommodations. I just want to be like the other kids. But I do like Mrs. Flores. She gives us "money" for working hard and then on a Friday we get to go shopping. She has all kinds of things like toys and Pokémon cards. I saved up my money and one day I bought half a dozen doughnuts!

I used to wear my jacket to school every day. Mom took it away from me because she said it was getting too warm to be wearing a jacket. I didn't want her to take it away. I used it at school. I wore the hood up all the time so I could hide. I walked with my head down and didn't look at anybody and hoped nobody could see me. It was warm and cozy and it helped me feel more comfortable and less afraid. Mom said I looked so sad all the time.

Our rental house isn't so bad. We aren't living out of boxes anymore and we get to ride our bikes to school. It is really hot and I get so mad at Lucy and Harrison for going so slow but I can get my frustration out when I ride. There are kids to play with and we get to go to the park whenever we want. Lucy's friend from school lives right across the street from us. And Harrison made a friend who lives on the street behind us. Aaron doesn't live that close so I can't play with him as much as Harrison gets to play with his friend. But they let me play too and it can be fun sometimes.

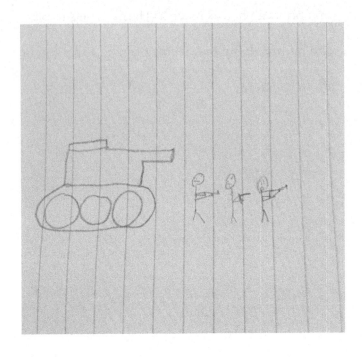

Mrs. C.

I wanted to give you an update on how Jackson has been doing this morning. We all know Mondays are usually the toughest days for him. He was refusing to do his work in the technology class. The teacher asked him to sign onto Study Island, he refused and closed the computer. I went in just to ask him to come sit with me and talk, then we could get him bac into class after technology ended. He refused. I gave him the choices to work on Study Island or come with me, and if no choice I would notify you on his behavior.

The behavior was not severe or disrupting, just defiant. I wanted to make sure I followed through and notified you. Jackson had wonderful days on Thursday and Friday. I checked in on his classroom and he was doing work and participating well throughout the day. I think Mondays are the toughest, and we will keep doing all we can here to pump him up an get him actively engaged at school.

We look forward to continuing to working alongside you to help Jackson. I'm hopeful he can turn it around today. Please let me know if you have any questions. Feel free to email me back or call me.

Mr. Woods

CHAPTER ELEVEN

It's my birthday. I am now ten years old. I didn't want a big party or anything. Plus with the new baby Mom couldn't plan a lot. And I don't have a lot of Friends anyway. We invited the friends I do have over for a stay late, we didn't even call it a birthday party. Nobody brought gifts. Aaron and his brother came.

So did Harrison's friend, Ben and another Jackson from church. We played video games and swam and ate tons of junk food and pizza. It was fun.

I have a behavior chart in school. It's part of my IEP. Each day my teacher keeps track of how well or how bad I did. It's supposed to help me. I don't understand why. It just makes me feel angry. I don't want to have a behavior chart, even if I get rewards for doing well. I don't want rewards. I just want to be like all the other kids. I'm not like other kids. I'm smart, I know I am but I can't show it like they do. I get so frustrated.

Reading is still hard. Math is easy. I want harder math. I'm not allowed to do harder math because they say I need to finish the work that I am given. I don't always finish math. I get frustrated because I know the answer but they want me to write it out and explain how I got it. Why do I need to do that if I got the answer right? Sometimes I get so frustrated I scribble on my paper or tear it up or crumple it in a ball. That's when I get in trouble. I don't get sent to the principal's office like I did last year unless I get three strikes on my behavior chart. It seems like I'm always in trouble or someone is always mad at me. I don't mean to get so angry. I don't mean to have a bad day. I want to have a good day. I want to do a good job. I try really hard, I really do. I just can't control myself. I don't even feel myself getting angry. I just explode.

I do like music this year. Last year I almost failed music class. I didn't want to sing or play instruments or do anything. I hated it. But this year is different.

My music teacher plays fun games with us. I don't know why but I like it now. Harrison is in band. He plays the trumpet. He really wanted to play the baritone but Mom convinced him to play the trumpet because it's smaller. The other day I told him, "Now I see why you wanted to play the baritone. To cover up your farts." That made everyone laugh.

A kid friendly Pompeii. An ice cream cone volcano, hot fudge river, sprinkle lava, gummy bear kids and a candy house.

Mrs. C,

It has been a challenge lately as Jackson has used a strong or forceful tone with me and his classmates. Today, he definitely did not want me to help him and he let me know with his words and body language (fisted hands, head down, not willing to respond at all at times). I just keep casually reminding him that I am happy to answer any questions or help him in any way I can. My hope, as well as the hope of the principal and the team, is that he will get started on the work when he feels ready. Unfortunately, that has not been happening yet but I will keep presenting the material and offering to help him. I truly appreciate all of your hard work in helping him stay up to date with his assignments.

Mrs. Jones

CHAPTER TWELVE

I was a Stormtrooper from Star Wars for Halloween. You know how we're not supposed to take candy from strangers? Does that apply on Halloween? I got to trick or treat with my friend Aaron. We got so much candy. I had lots to give to the Great Pumpkin. Every year we leave the majority of our candy out for the "Great Pumpkin" (like in Charlie Brown). He takes our candy and leaves us a toy or something cool.

I told Mom I'm sad I'm never going to be able to

bob for apples. She asked why. I told her because my name isn't Bob. The only thing I will ever be able to do is Jackson for apples.

Our baby, Calvin, is trying to roll over. He's so chubby and cute. He's a happy baby. I'm glad he doesn't cry a lot. He likes to laugh and blow raspberries. He's super ticklish under his chin.

My feet are now as big as Mom's and the same size as Harrison's. Mom sometimes wears our flip flops. The other day she wore them to take us to school. When Lucy saw her wearing Harrison's flip flops she said, "So Harrison is a full grown woman now?!" Sometimes Lucy can be funny.

There is one thing I love and no matter what kind of day I have I always get to go. Scouts. I've been in Cub Scouts since I was eight. When I turn eleven I will be a Boy Scout. We have scouts every Wednesday. Mom will not take that away from me. Last year when I was getting in trouble a lot and coming home with the work I didn't finish at school Mom and Dad would threaten to take away wrestling. I wrestle in spring time. I love to wrestle, I like it more than swimming. Dad said that athletes in high school have to keep good grades or they don't get to play and maybe we should start that now. Mom says she will still take me to wrestling and I can just bring my homework. Then when my homework is done I can join the practice. I don't think I ever finished my work so fast. But I was mad. I hate being late and they started as I was finishing. Mom said I finished right on time but it still felt like I was late. They don't do that with scouts. Mom said she will never keep me from going to scouts. Dad was an Eagle Scout and I want to be one too.

When I started scouts at eight years old I went to a day camp and was given a baby Beta fish. It was so small it could barely eat the food we gave it. I named it Bob. After all this time I still have Bob. Harrison was given a Beta fish at the same day camp and even thought his was bigger than mine his didn't live that long. Lucy even got a Beta fish from the pet store one time. Hers died after a while but I still have mine. Good old Bob.

I started going with Mom to school meetings about me. I want to know what they are saying and I want to help make decisions. It's about me so why wouldn't I want to be there? My teachers and principal were surprised the first time I showed up at one of the meetings. I must have done something right because at the end of the meeting they thanked me for coming and said they were pleased that I would take ownership like that. Whatever that means. I just want to know what they are saying about me.

Mrs. Jones,

Thanks for keeping me updated. I kind of "laid down the law" today and told Jackson he is expected to do three things:

Start work immediately

Be respectful (no saying I don't want to, saying yes please and no thank you, using a respectful voice, etc.)

Do his best work

I explained that he obviously has not learned how to work so if he is unable to work at school he will have to work on that skill at home. I made a list of extra chores and jobs that he can do at home to help teach him work ethics, on top of any work he doesn't not complete at school.

This is the first talk I have had with him that he hasn't complained or back talked. I'm really hopeful! On Monday he had to finish his class work before starting wrestling. We took his work and he finished while waiting to start. I explained that he has all day at school to work and if he chooses not to use that time he has to give something gup to make up for that. I finally found a way to put the ball in his court because I am not taking wrestling away from him, he is losing wrestling time because he chose to waste time at school.

Mrs. C.

CHAPTER THIRTEEN

Christmas was pretty great. One of the best things was getting two weeks off of school. I got a paintball gun for Christmas. I love paintball. I like to play Capture the Flag with paintball. Mom gave each of us a box of cereal. She never, I mean never, buys sugary cereal, except for Christmas. She wraps our favorite cereal and puts it under the tree then we get to eat it for our Christmas breakfast.

After Christmas we went to the sand dunes for a couple of days. It was nice and all but we didn't get as much time playing with all our new presents. It is fun to ride the sand rail though.

When we got home from the sand dunes my Mom's sisters came to visit. All of them. She has six sisters. Most of my cousins were here too and of course Grammy and Grampy, Mom's mom and dad. It was fun and crowded and busy. Most of Mom's sisters live out of state so we don't see them much. Grammy had a party for all the cousins. Grampy dressed up like Santa. We call him Santa Grampy. Later we had a white elephant gift exchange with everyone. A white elephant gift is a gift that nobody really wants. We went to a thrift store and found funny gifts then wrapped them and played the game. I really liked the toilet night light I got.

Mom forced us to take family pictures with everyone. I had to wear nice clothes, I thought what I had was nice enough but Mom didn't think so and made me change. We spent a lot of time playing with our cousins at the park by our house. Lucy especially loved having our cousins visit. She wants a sister so bad she liked having all the girl cousins stay with us. It was a good Christmas break.

It's February and we finally sold our house! It took forever. Mom and Dad were starting to get worried. Paying a mortgage and rent was starting to be too much. We wouldn't have had this problem if we never would have moved. I liked our old house.

Mom and Dad asked what we could do to help save money. We decided as a family to stop eating out until our house sold. We went more than two months without eating at a restaurant so we could save money. When our house sold we went out for dinner.

Mrs. C.

Today Jackson struggled a bit and had several instances where he told me and other students "no" and/or was not using respectful words/tone with others. I reminded him how important that is as his peers were having a difficult time with how he was communicating with them. He was able to get through tasks in class with only a few reminders.

Mrs. Jones

CHAPTER FOURTEEN

I got suspended from school. A three day
suspension. All for asking a question. I wanted to go
home so I asked my teacher if we could pack up yet. I
didn't get a good answer so I asked again. And then I
got sent to the principal's office and got suspended.
Mom and Dad agreed with the principal. They

thought I should be suspended. When I asked why Mom said it's because I scared my teacher. She said I followed my teacher around the classroom asking again and again if I could go home and wouldn't listen to any directions. All I wanted was to go home. I wouldn't have followed my teacher asking her questions if she had answered me. Mom said she did give me an answer but because I didn't like it I asked again and again. She said I followed close behind my teacher and made it difficult for her to walk. She said I became hostile and it was scary for my teacher and the other students. I still say it wasn't my fault.

School is awful and I hate it. It's so hard and I can't do anything right. But it's also boring because I'm not challenged at all. It's weird. Reading and writing is so hard but what we are learning is so easy.

Mom started tutoring me again. She asked what would help me in school. I said to read better. Mom asked if it would help if I got extra tutoring. I said we could try. So she's tutoring me at school again. I'm glad. I don't have to do reading with my class anymore because that does not help at all. I like seeing Mom during school.

Sometimes when I get frustrated at school I will slam my chair against the floor. I used to hit it against the wall until my teacher moved me. We set it as a goal not to do that. I don't do it on purpose, I just get so mad and I lose control.

We had another meeting at school. We've had so many and it's always about my behavior. We set new goals. My goals include not breaking pencils or tearing

up paper, erasures, stress balls or other objects.
Keeping my chair flat on the ground. No crumbling
up papers and throwing them. And to follow
directions. Same as always, but I am being held more
accountable. I get points when I get through a
subject, like math or science, without doing those
things. I get more points for using positive strategies
like taking a break with Mrs. Flores, using a stress ball
or a colored overly to help me read. At the end of the
day if I've earned enough points I get a reward.
I asked why I have to do this. Mrs. Flores said it's so
they can track my progress. She showed me all the
data they collected and put in a chart to mark my
progress. I guess that's alright.

After we set my goals my teacher asked if I
remembered the hamster I told her about. I saw a

hamster at the pet store and thought it would be nice to have in class. Animals calm me down and if I had a hamster I could visit it when I felt upset. She said she spoke with the principal and she agreed to let me have a class pet if I can meet my goals from now until spring break. It's only a few weeks. I'm going to work super hard.

I've worked really hard for the past couple of weeks. It's been exhausting. Reading and writing take three times the effort for me than it does for other people. By the end of each day I am so tired. Other kids don't get so tired from school but I do, my brain is working harder than theirs.

Mrs. C.

Today Jackson had some struggles with ow he spoke with me and others. I did need to ask for some assistance and he had some breaks in the front office as you know. Jackson did not complete his assignments in class so I did send them home in his back pack when you picked him up today.

Earlier today as I put items in the folder in his cubby Jackson gave me back the blue folder an said he would not do the assignments. A suggestion was made by my instructional coach to send home any future work with his brother. We are at the end of the school year but are still working on new concepts so I will continue to send home items that are not completed for you to see what we are working on. I will try and send the items home with his brother if needed.

Mrs. Jones

CHAPTER FIFTEEN

I started wrestling. I love wrestling. I like it better than swim. It helps me get my frustrations out. I wish I could do it all year but they only have it in the spring. I was working on a book report and was getting angry and frustrated. I'm surprised Mom let me go to wrestling without it being finished because it was due the next day. I went to wrestling and when I came home I sat down and finished my project super-fast. For some reason wrestling helps me think better.

For spring break we went to Rocky Point,

Mexico. The beaches are rocky, the water is shallow and I didn't like all the crabs and stuff. Hermit crabs scare me. Harrison loves them but I hate them. The rest of the trip was fun, like the shopping and the Mexican candy store and the piñata. I loved the mangoes they sold on the beach. They peeled and cut them for you. They were so sweet and juicy.

We had another school meeting. The principal said it was a celebratory meeting because I met my goal! I did everything I was supposed to do for those weeks before spring break. This time instead of talking about what I do wrong we talked about what I did right. Everyone there, my teacher, Mrs. Flores and the principal clapped for me because I earned my hamster! Mom took me to the pet store as soon as I got out of school. I chose a winter white dwarf hamster. I named her Gidget. I wanted to name her

Voldemort but she's a girl not a boy. Lucy said that would be awkward and suggested Hermione Granger. I thought Granger was a good name. Then Mom said Granger reminds her of Gidget and I like that even better. So I named her Gidget. We get to keep her at home for a week while we take standardized tests at school so she won't be a distraction and to help her get used to her new cage. She is the best hamster ever. She is soft and white with gray on her back. She doesn't hide when she sees me, she comes to me and wants to sniff me and eats from my hand and lets me pet and hold her. I was so worried I would mess up and then I wouldn't be able to get a hamster. I worked so hard. I came home from school every day exhausted because I was trying so hard to meet my goals. I can't believe I did it. I can't believe I earned Gidget! I am responsible for her. Feeding her and cleaning her cage and keeping Barkley away from her. I will take her to school on Mondays where she will stay all week until I bring her home on Fridays. She's the best thing that has happened to me in a long time.

Hi Jackson,

I missed seeing you today! You make my day when you come in for breaks!

I wanted to just let you know that you can always come to me and ask or tell me anything. I know you are very, very intelligent and can accurately assume the answer to some questions based on the facts given to you, however, I am always open to hear you out and come up with a compromise if possible.

I completely understand not wanting to miss the fun opportunities in class. I don't want you or any of my students to miss things like that. I know since you went up yesterday and Friday is my only day to make-up groups that you thought there wasn't flexibility in the schedule to make-up additional time. If you come to me and express yourself like you did yesterday, I promise to do everything in my power to work it out! I am here to help you. I am not against you. Again, I promise to always hear you out, but I can't hear your point-of-view if you don't come to me and express them. My Jedi senses are good, but I'm still mastering that concept!

I see your potential Jackson. You are an amazing kid! I'm not sure if you read some of the signs in our classroom but the one says "365 Days, 365 Chances". Tomorrow is a new day! And remember my classroom is a safe place. I'm sure you notice the amount of students that are in and out throughout the day because they feel safe coming to my classroom to celebrate, learn, be sad, and even get pretty angry sometimes. Please know you can do the same if you want to.

Please come see me during your first break so we can come up with a plan. Sleep tight my young Jedi!

Love,

Mrs. Flores

CHAPTER SIXTEEN

I'm done with tutoring and I'm done with counseling and I'm done with school. It actually turned out to be a good year. Well the end was good. Gidget made it good.

Its summer. Lucy and I are doing swim team again. This year Mom is making Lucy do the swim meets.

The other day Mom told me to go ask Dad if he needed any help. I said, "I think Dad's in the bathroom and I DON'T want to ask him if he needs any help." That made Mom laugh really hard.

We went on a family trip. A ten day road trip to San Francisco and down to Los Angeles and then back home to Phoenix. We've never done a big trip like that with just our family. Mom has taken us kids to Idaho to visit our cousins and we have gone on some trips with Dad's family but never one this big with just us. And Marlie, Dad's little sister. She's 15 and we are exactly alike. Mom says we have the same sense of humor, we say funny things all the time.

We did all kinds of stuff on our trip We went to Pier 29 in San Francisco and went in a mirror maze. The funniest part was when Harrison thought he saw the way out and started running but ran right into a mirror. We laughed so hard. Harrison got a bloody nose and a fat lip but we couldn't stop laughing. He was a good sport about it.

I also liked the candy shop we went to. But let me warn you, chocolate covered bacon is disgusting. My favorite was Knott's Berry Farm. That place is awesome. Marlie and I went on every ride there. Even the big, big ones. I also liked boogie boarding in the ocean. We ate mangoes that people walking the beach sold and we all got sunburned.

As soon as we got back from our trip we had to move again. I hate moving. Mom and Dad bought a house because the rental house we were in kicked us out. The owner decided to sell the house and so we couldn't live there anymore. We bought a house just down the street and around the corner. It's ok because I really like the house we just moved into even though I hate moving. Harrison and I have our own rooms for the first time ever. Mom and Dad bought us new beds and gave me a desk. I got to set up my room just the way I like and nobody can go in unless I say. I can play Legos as much as I want without anyone messing them up. And I can listen to whatever I choose to. I like to listen to audiobooks. I love audiobooks, they let me enjoy books instead of feeling stupid because I can't read them. Harrison loves going to the library and the bookstore. I hate it. It makes me feel stupid seeing all those books I can't read. But now I have my own cd player in my room and can listen to all the audiobooks I want.

Calvin turned one. Even though we just moved

in last week we had a birthday party for him. He went crazy over his birthday cake. He picked the whole thing up and started eating it. He cried when it fell on his lap. Mom picked it back up and handed it to him and he was happy again. He kept saying "mmmmmm" and would stop and clap his hands. Afterwards, he was a mess! I'm glad I didn't have to clean him up.

Calvin is walking everywhere and getting into everything. He doesn't talk yet but he knows some signs. Eat, more, finished, milk.

On Monday school started again. I'm in 5th grade. Harrison is in 7th and Lucy is in 3rd. I'm excited and nervous at the same time. Excited because I love to learn. Nervous because who wouldn't be if they had dyslexia?

It's still so hot and we don't have a pool to cool off in anymore so Mom has been taking us and picking us up from school. I don't know why schools start in August in Arizona. I mean it's the hottest month of the year and we live in the hottest state too. We should start later when it's cooler and we don't have to stay in our classrooms during recess.

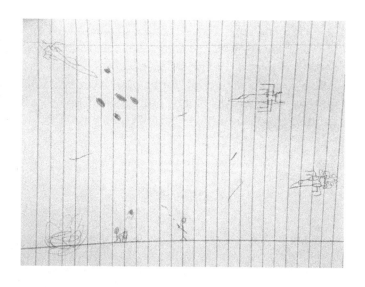

Mrs. C.

He's had an incredible couple of weeks, so I'm hoping tomorrow will be a great day! He really has been doing good, I think sometimes his frustrations take over his ability to ask for help, so we're working on that. We've made a lot of progress and we will continue to push through! Thank you for your support!!!

Mrs. Jones

CHAPTER SEVENTEEN

I don't know why but school is easier this year. I'm not angry like I used to be. I don't lose my temper and get mad like I used to. I still have a hard time reading but with all the help I got from Mrs. Flores I'm doing much better. I still go to her room for reading help. I have homework every night this year. It's always a math worksheet. I'm good at math so I don't mind my homework. I even do it without Mom asking. But I do ask her help reading the word problems. It's such a change from last year and every year before that. I used to get so frustrated and angry and lose my temper. I felt like I had no control. I didn't want to get mad, I would try not to but then I would just explode. Third grade was even worse. I wore my jacket all the time and kept my hood up. I didn't look at anyone and barely spoke. When I did I was very quiet. Everything was hard and frustrating. I felt so lonely and sad. I haven't felt sad at all in fifth grade.

Even though I'm in a new class room and new grade and have a new teacher, I still get to take Gidget to school with me. I take her in on Mondays and leave her at school until Friday when I take her home and clean her cage.

I made up a song. "we're following the leader" from Peter Pan and then changed the words to "we're passing the gas, the gas, the gas. We're passing the gas wherever we may go"

Sometimes I wonder, are slugs just homeless snails?

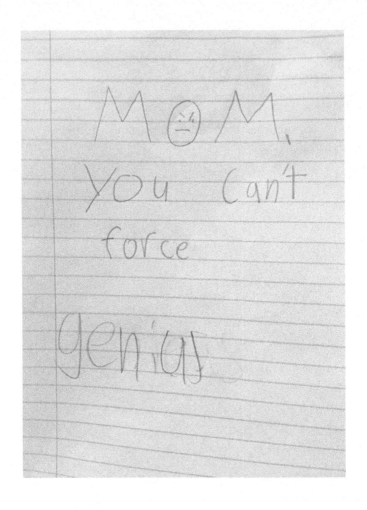

Dear Mrs. C.

AS we end this school year, I have to share… When I first met Jackson, I immediately saw his potential. I knew he was going to do amazing things because he is so brilliant, but I saw his potential to love school, love life, and love himself. The more I got to know Jackson, the more I wanted this for him. I could not be more proud of his hard-work and effort this school year. I am excited for next school year and his continued progress!

I know, as a teacher, I am not supposed to have favorites. I honestly do love all of my students! As much as I love each of them, I can still tell you that Jackson is my favorite! I can't help it! You have raised a pretty incredible kid! Jackson has made my day on so many different occasions and I don't think he even realizes it. I can't imagine this school year without him as one of my students. He changed it for the better, for sure!

Thank you for sharing him! I hope you guys have a great summer!

Mrs. Flores

CHAPTER EIGHTEEN

I can't believe it. I made Student of the Month! I have always wanted to be student of the month. I was hoping so bad I would get it. The last two months of school last year I tried really hard to get student of the month. I worked hard and improved so much I thought for sure I would be chosen. I was really disappointed when I wasn't. But I got it for the first time ever. What makes it better is I got it the first month of school. Out of all the kids in my class my teacher chose me! Mom and Mrs. Flores cried when they found out. I was just happy. I got a certificate

(Lucy used to call them "terificates") and was recognized at our school assembly. There were treats for all the kids who made student of the month and their parents after the assembly. Mom and even Mrs. Flores wanted pictures of me. Mom walked me to class after that. Of course all the kids went crazy over Calvin. Mom asked my teacher if she knew how bad I wanted student of the month. My teacher said no, she chose me because out of all the kids in her class I deserved it. I am the one who works the hardest and stays on task. She knew I've struggled in school but all she has seen is how hard I am working. It feels good to be recognized.

Mom always writes different quotes on a chalkboard in our house. I came up with one of my own. "Good is not good enough. Great is great enough." I want to be great.

I'm starting my own company. I want to make and sell t-shirts. I have lots of good ideas. One of the shirts I made has a picture of Luke Skywalker and Darth Vader that says "best friends". It's funny because they really aren't best friends. Another shirt I made has a little monster coming out of the pocket. One of them has a picture of a person hanging off a cliff. It says "just hang in there".

CHAPTER NINETEEN

I'm eleven now. This year I did have a big party. It was a Star Wars party. I invited lots of friends. We had all kinds of junk food and we gave them all Star Wars names. Lightsaber red vines, Death Star Doughnuts, Hans Rolos, Yoda Soda, BB8 Popcorn Balls, Vader Ade, Luke Skywater, Padawan Popcorn. We ate Tatooine Tacos for dinner. We decorated and used black star shaped paper plates. We hung a sign on the bathroom door that had a picture of Han Solo that said, "Don't forget to wash your Hans". We played Star Wars video games, had a lightsaber fight

and a silly string war. I got lots of gifts, gift cards,

candy and Star Wars stuff. Harrison spent his

very own money and bought me the best gift. An

iPod. He says it's so I can listen to audiobooks

anytime I want to. Every friend I invited, except two,

came. There were 12 kids plus me, Harrison and

Lucy. I can't believe I have so many friends.

Mom heard about this thing on the radio where I

can try to be the State Fair Kid Correspondent. I

definitely want to be the kid correspondent. I want to

be an actor so this would be a great way to start. All I

have to do is write why I want to be the kid

correspondent in 200 words or less. It's still hard for

me to write but I'm learning different strategies . I

dictated and Mom typed for me. Here's what I wrote;

You should select me as the Arizona State Fair Kid Correspondent because it sounds like fun and is a great opportunity to show the state who I really am. I am Jackson. I'm a 5th grader. I have dyslexia and I want to show every kid out there that anything can happen no matter what their challenges are. I could only read a few words when I was in third grade. I got in trouble a lot because I kept asking the teacher to read for me. Then I was diagnosed with dyslexia and got help with reading from a teacher who believed in me. Now, I can read so much better, I'm happier and I don't get into trouble any more. I was even made student of the month. I want all kids to know that no matter what challenges they have they can always do great things.

I didn't win. But even without winning I don't feel so different anymore.

ABOUT THE AUTHOR

Kendra Cuzick enjoys cookies and a good nap. Her favorite job has been teaching preschool. She is currently going back to school for a degree in neuropsychology. Kendra lives in Phoenix Arizona with her husband and five children.

KENDRA CUZICK